W9-DDL-860

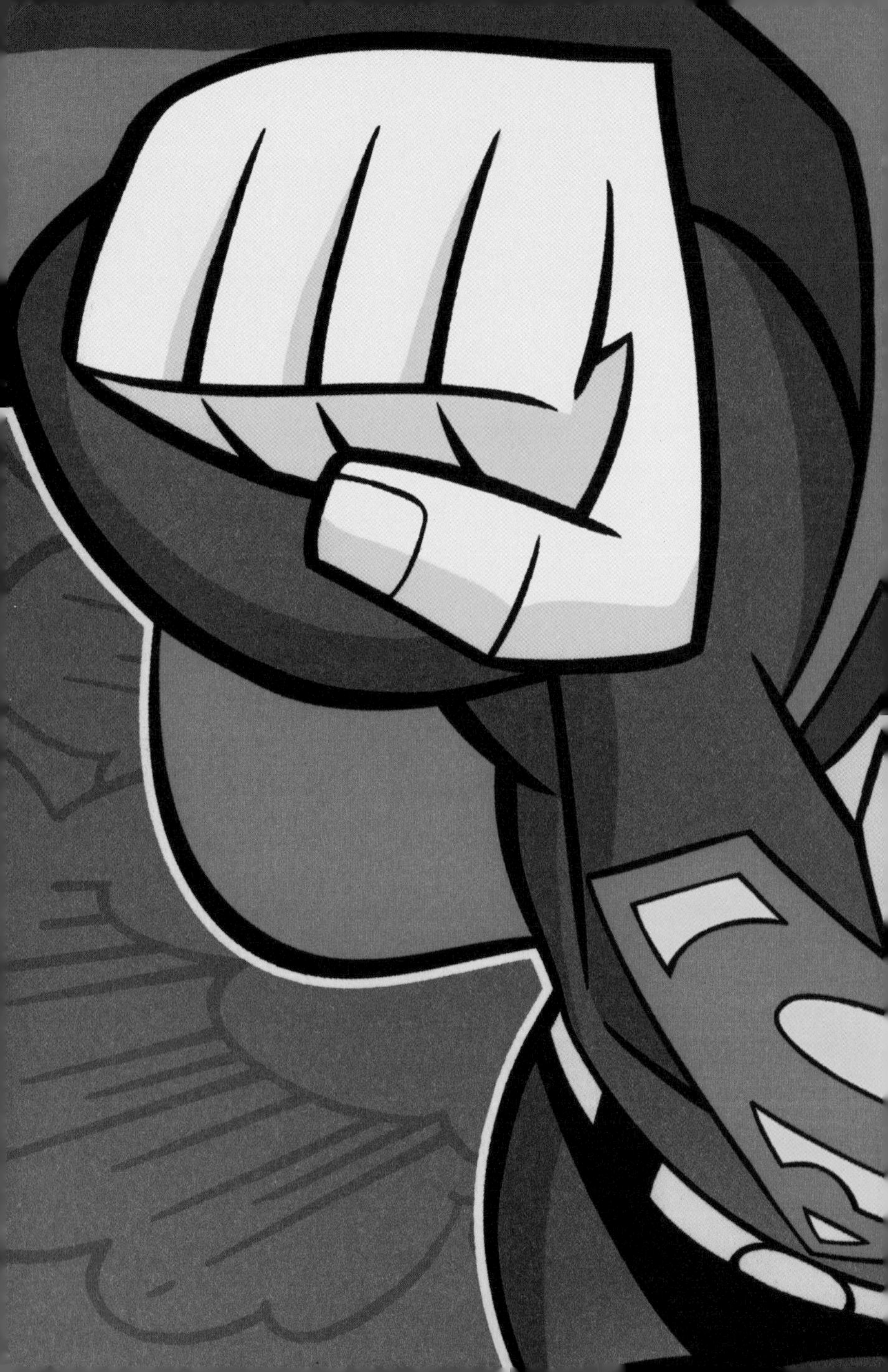

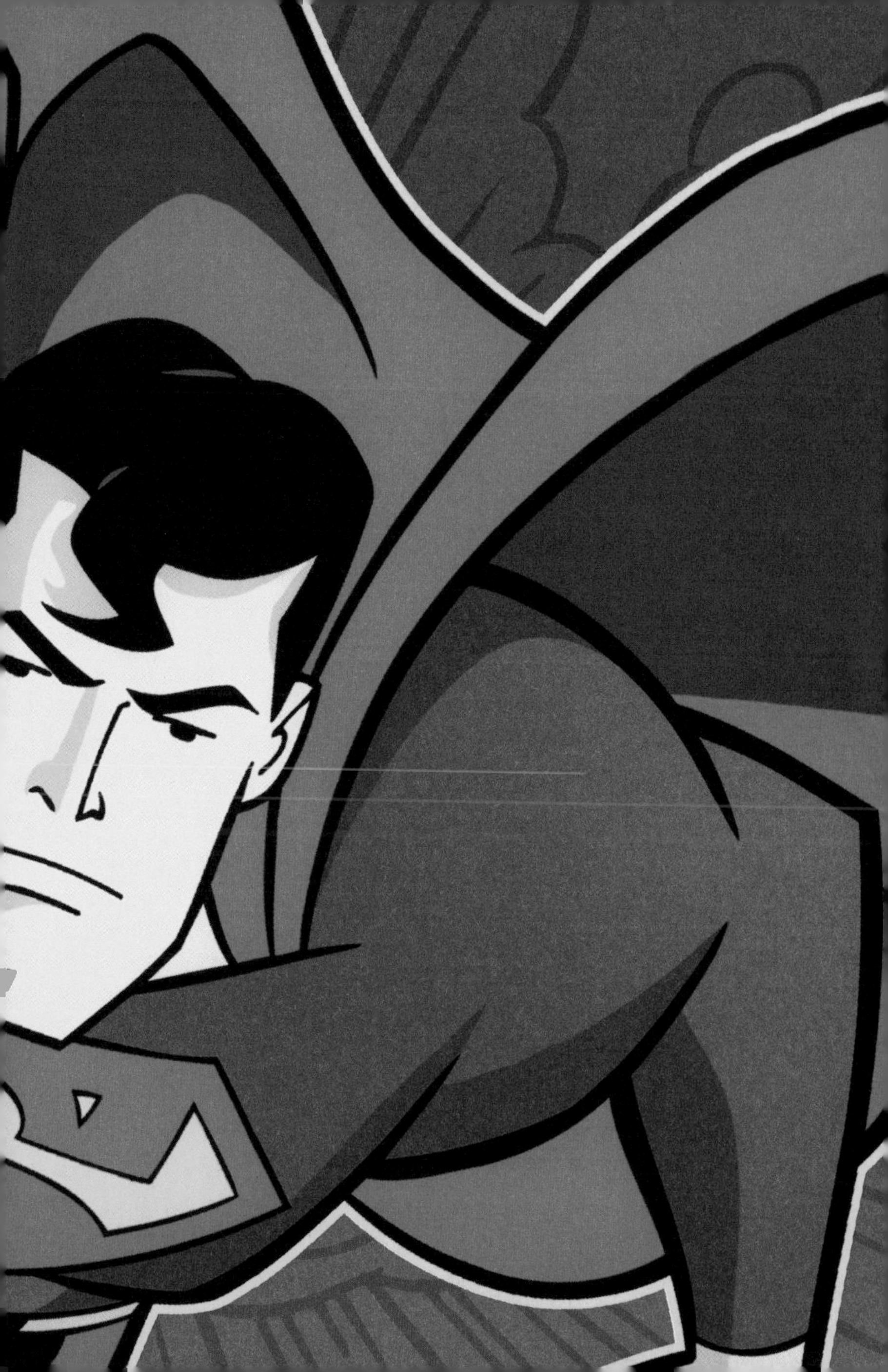

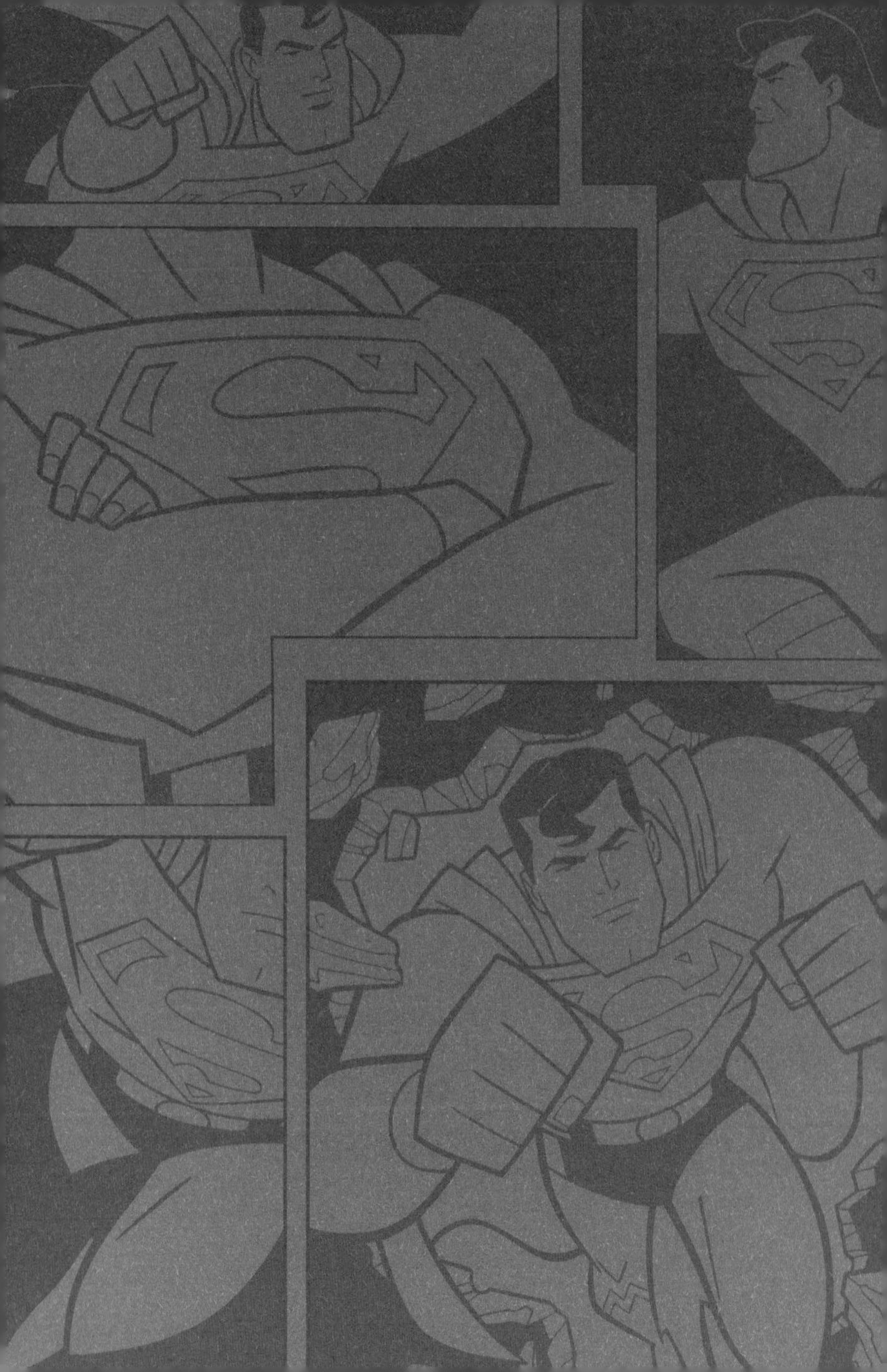

SUPER DC HEROES

SUPERMAN™

DEEP SPACE HIJACK

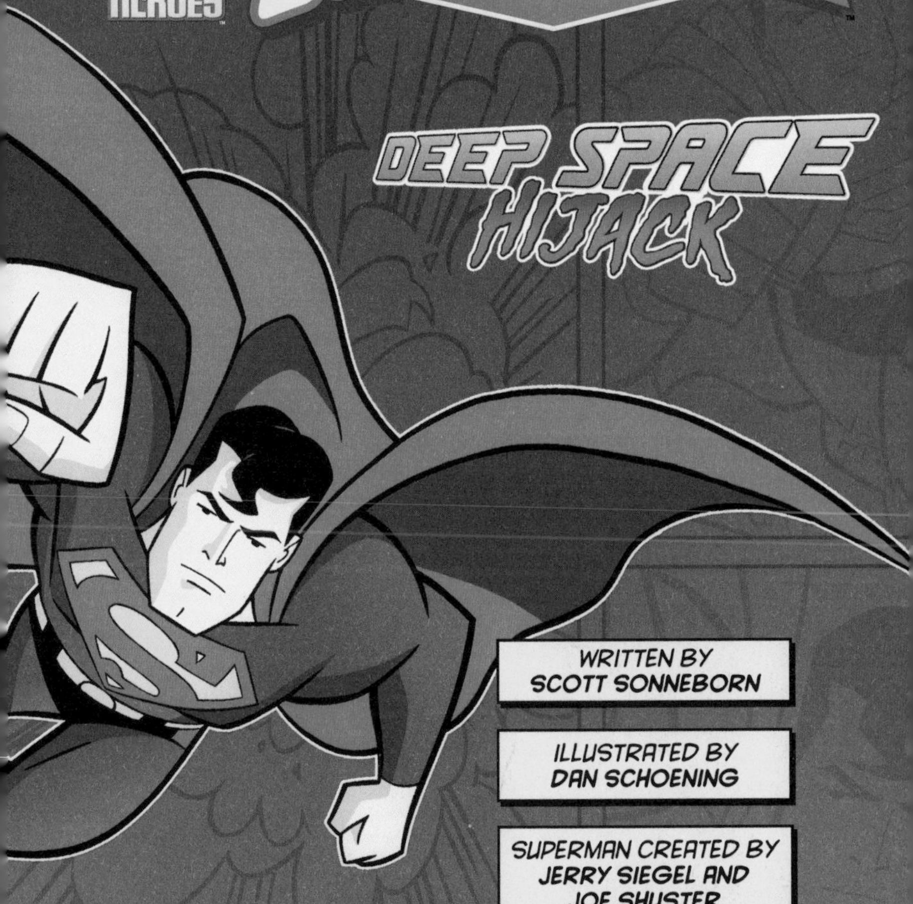

WRITTEN BY
SCOTT SONNEBORN

ILLUSTRATED BY
DAN SCHOENING

SUPERMAN CREATED BY
JERRY SIEGEL AND
JOE SHUSTER

STONE ARCH BOOKS
a capstone imprint

Published by Stone Arch Books in 2010
A Capstone Imprint
151 Good Counsel Drive, P.O. Box 669
Mankato, Minnesota 56002
www.capstonepub.com

Library of Congress Cataloging-in-Publication Data

Sonneborn, Scott.
  Deep space hijack / by Scott Sonneborn ; illustrated by Dan Schoening
    p. cm. -- (DC super heroes, Superman)
  ISBN 978-1-4342-1880-3 (library binding) -- ISBN 978-1-4342-2257-2
(pbk.)
  [1. Superheroes--Fiction.] I. Schoening, Dan, ill. II. Title.
  PZ7.7.S646Dee 2010
  [Fic]--dc22
                                    2009029327

Summary: When astronauts crash on Pluto, only one man can save
them . . . Superman! Faster than a speeding bullet, the Man of Steel soars
toward the dwarf planet, towing a high-tech rescue vehicle. Soon, he
discovers an unexpected passenger aboard the spacecraft. Jimmy Olsen,
the *Daily Planet*'s young photographer, has hitched a ride, but that's not
Superman's biggest problem. When the evil Kanjar Ro attacks, the Man
of Steel finds himself weakened by deep-space travel. Can he summon the
strength to defeat the alien invader 3,660,000,000 miles from Earth's yellow
sun?

Art Director: Bob Lentz
Designer: Hilary Wacholz
Production Specialist: Michelle Biedscheid

Printed in the United States of America in Stevens Point, Wisconsin.
092009
005619WZS10

TABLE OF CONTENTS

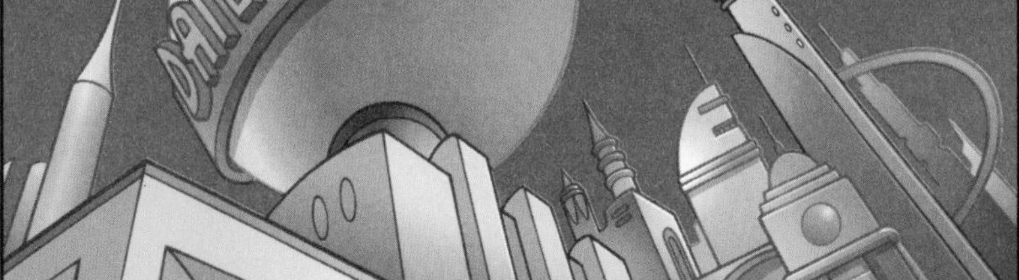

DAILY PLANET

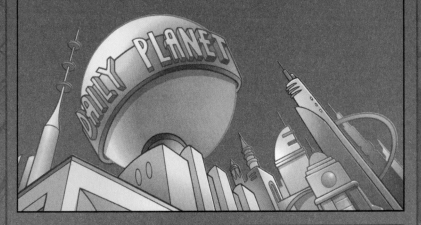

CHAPTER 1

EMERGENCY IN DEEP SPACE

The Long Range Space Explorer had just returned to the solar system. The spacecraft was approaching Pluto, when suddenly —

"We've lost engines!" cried the ship's copilot.

"Prepare for emergency landing," said Captain Tully, the astronaut in command of the Long Range Explorer.

"Where?" panicked the copilot. "We're still three trillion miles from Earth!"

"That doesn't change the fact that our hyperdrive engines are dead," replied the captain. "We have to land this spacecraft right now!"

Captain Tully flicked on the intercom. "All hands," he called out in the calmest voice that he could. "Prepare for impact . . . on Pluto!"

*   *   *

"I've got a great idea," Jimmy Olsen whispered to Clark Kent.

Clark and Jimmy were sitting in the lobby of the S.T.A.R. Labs Space Center. S.T.A.R.'s Long Range Space Explorer had just made an emergency landing on Pluto. As a reporter for the *Daily Planet* newspaper, Clark had come for the scoop. Jimmy tagged along as his photographer, but he seemed more interested in other things.

Clark sighed. "Whenever you have a 'great idea,' it only means one thing," he told Jimmy. "Trouble!"

"Oh, you sound just like Superman," replied Jimmy. "He always tells me that."

Jimmy didn't know how right he was. Nobody knew it, but Clark Kent was secretly the Man of Steel.

Clark and Jimmy were waiting for someone at the Space Center to tell them what was happening on Pluto. At the moment, all the scientists were busy trying to find a way to rescue the astronauts.

While they were waiting, Jimmy figured he might as well look around.

"Come on, Mr. Kent," said Jimmy. He snuck up to a door marked 'Astronauts Only Beyond This Point.'

"I've always wanted to be an astronaut," Jimmy said. "This is probably as close as I'm ever going to get. I just want a peek."

"Wait," whispered Clark, but it was too late. Jimmy had slipped inside and shut the door behind him.

Clark shook his head. Jimmy Olsen often stuck his nose where it didn't belong. That made him good at getting photographs for the *Daily Planet*, but it made him even better at getting into trouble.

Clark stood up to follow Jimmy. Just then, a group of scientists hurried down the hall, followed by a gray-haired general.

"Out of my way!" the gruff general said to Clark. "We've got an emergency here!"

The general turned to the scientists behind him.

"Why in the world haven't you launched the rescue ship?" the general roared. "Those astronauts on Pluto only have two hours of air left. We're running out of time!"

The general and the scientists pushed past Clark into a room marked 'Mission Control.' They shut the door in Clark's face.

Clark pressed his nose up to the glass-paneled door. Inside, he saw a room filled with hundreds of computers and giant display screens. A dozen scientists stood around the general.

"No rocket can get the rescue ship to Pluto in a matter of hours," one of the scientists told the general. "Nothing on Earth can help them."

"I'm sorry," a voice called out, "but I have to disagree."

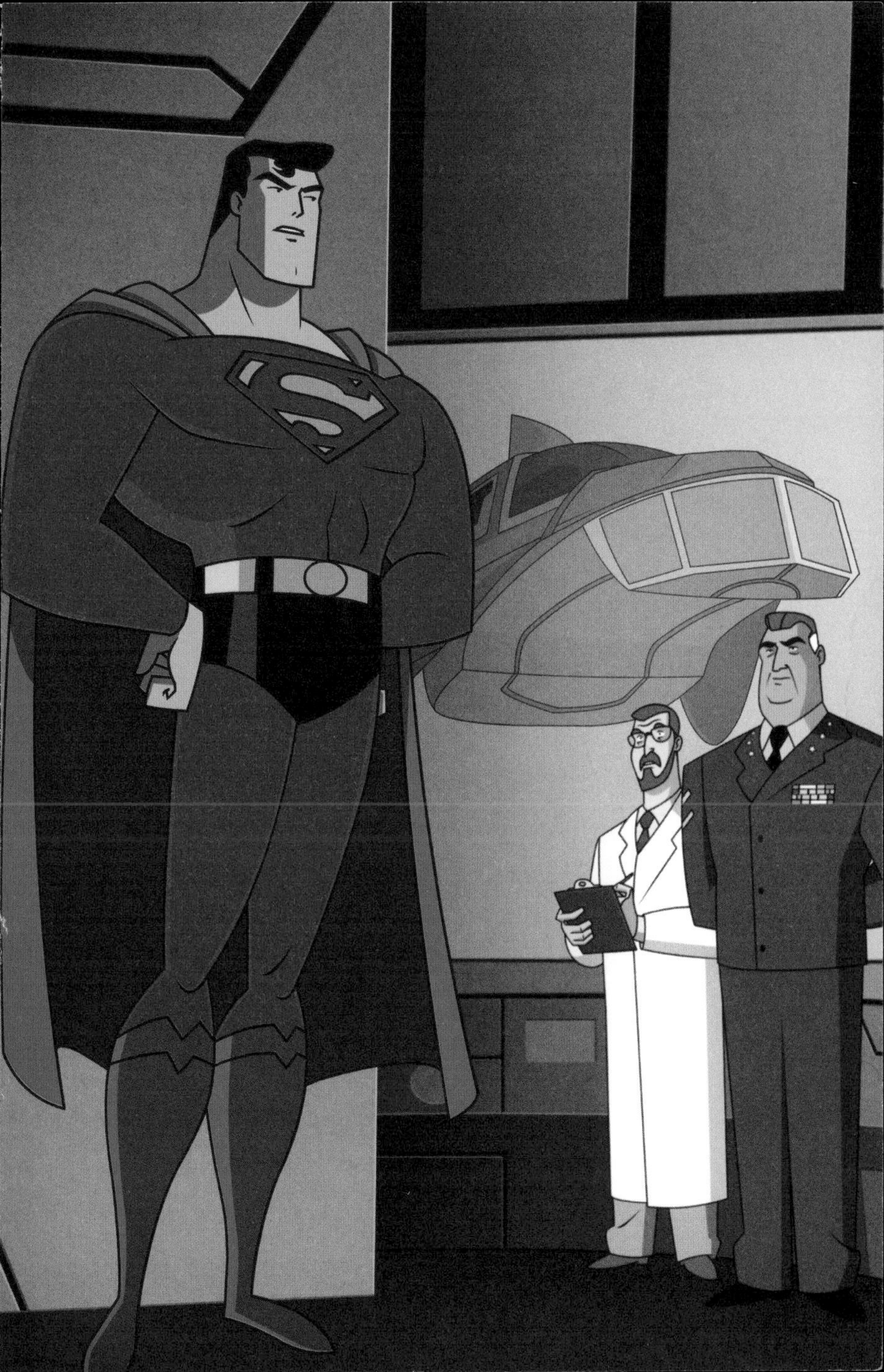

Everyone in the room turned to see that the voice belonged to Superman!

"I can carry the rescue ship," offered Superman. "If I fly at full speed, I'll be able to get to Pluto in time."

"Wow!" said a scientist. "We're lucky you showed up!"

It wasn't luck, thought the Man of Steel. *I overheard you and grabbed my spacesuit. Then I changed from Clark Kent into Superman at the speed of light!* Of course, he couldn't say that out loud — not without everyone learning his secret identity.

"This is no time for chit-chat!" the general roared at the scientist. "Superman's got some astronauts to save. Let's go!"

Outside, the rescue ship towered over the launch pad.

Superman ran his hand over the ship's hull. It was coated with an experimental metal called Leadellium. The alloy was nearly indestructible. That meant the rescue ship could go anywhere in the solar system: the molten core of Jupiter, the frozen wastes of Pluto, and even the center of the sun.

Leadellium was heavy. The rescue ship weighed over four million pounds. But Superman hardly seemed to notice as he lifted it onto his shoulders.

"Please bring them home safe, Superman," said the general. He sounded far less angry than before.

Superman nodded. "I won't let them down," he said. Bending his knees, Superman braced himself. Then he flew up into the air, propelling the massive rescue ship ahead of him.

ZWWWWOOOOMMMMM!

Superman flew faster and faster into the sky. Within seconds, the Space Center was just a tiny dot on the ground below him. He continued on, pushing the spacecraft through the clouds and into outer space.

If all goes according to plan, thought Superman, *I'll get the empty rescue ship to Pluto in just under two hours.*

Already, though, something was wrong. Someone had stowed aboard the rescue ship!

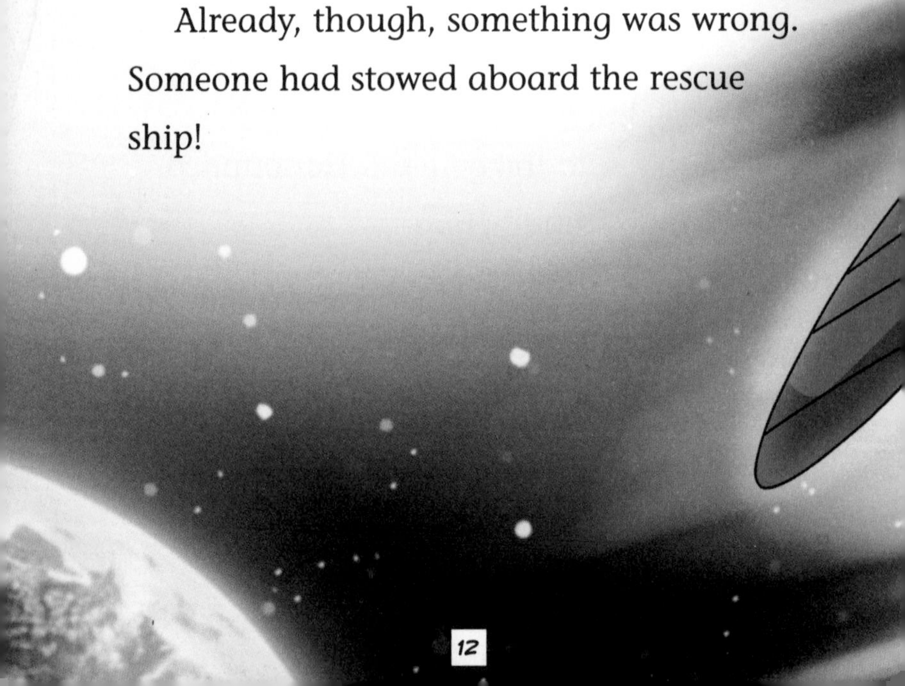

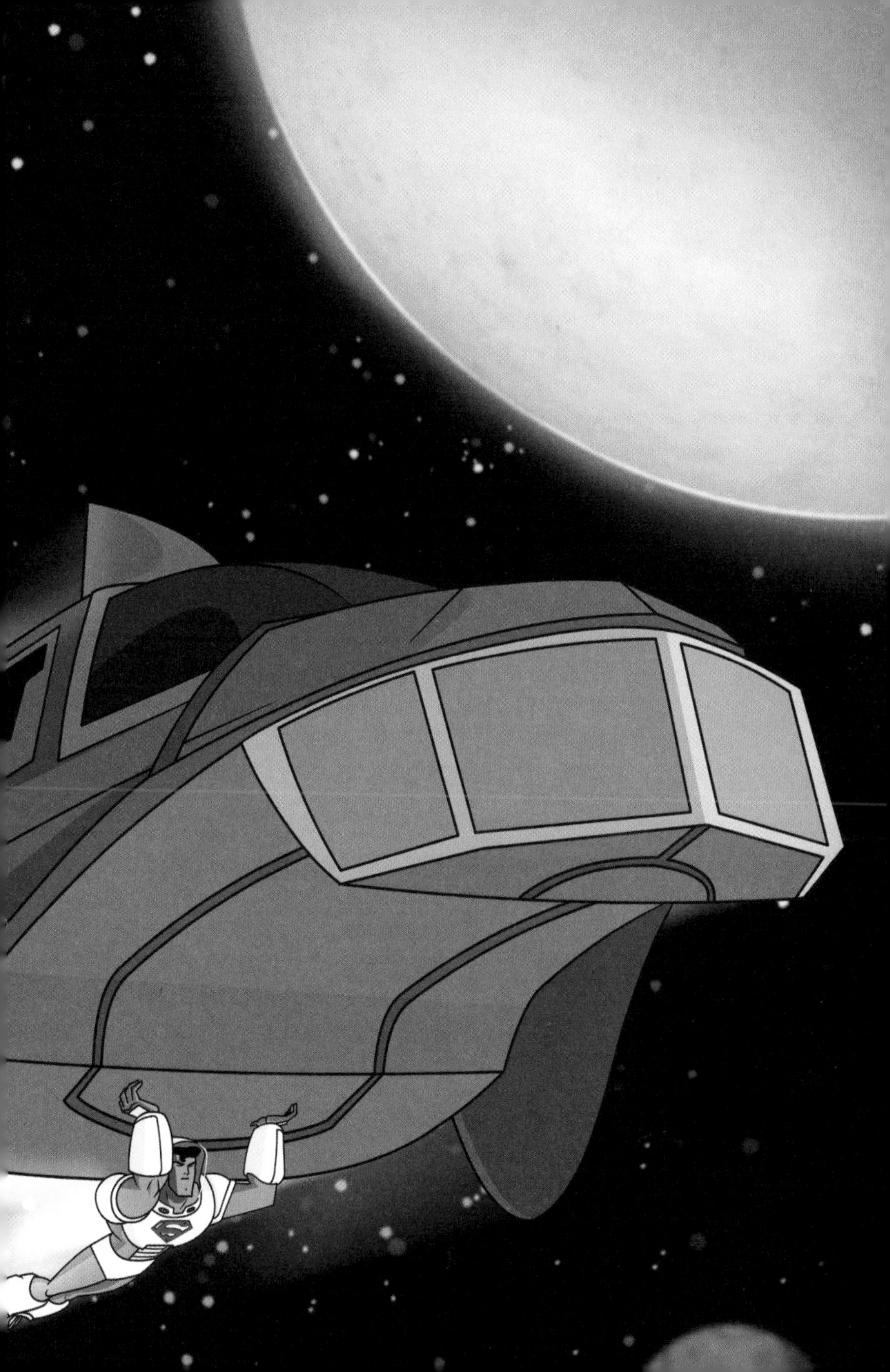

CHAPTER 2

THE STOWAWAY

Superman couldn't see inside the ship because Leadellium blocked his X-ray vision, but with his super-hearing he could tell someone was definitely onboard.

Superman didn't know who, and he didn't have time to check. He had to keep pushing the rescue ship as fast as he could to get to Pluto on time. He just hoped whoever was in the ship didn't know that.

"I know you're in there," Superman shouted. His voice was so loud, it could be heard inside the ship.

"Surrender now," Superman continued, "or I'll come in there and make you wish you had!"

"I give up!" squeaked a tiny voice from inside the ship.

Superman couldn't believe his ears. The stowaway on the rescue ship was Jimmy!

"Let me guess," said Superman. "Another one of your 'great ideas?'"

"No, this isn't a great idea," answered Jimmy. "It's my greatest! I'm actually in outer space!"

Superman was about to answer when suddenly, the dark of space lit up in a burst of color. FLASH! Superman looked up to see an enormous alien warship firing at them.

They were under attack!

"Earth is bad for business," yelled Kanjar Ro from inside the ship that was attacking Superman and Jimmy. Kanjar was an alien space pirate. He had a face like a dead fish, and his personality was just as slimy.

"There's nothing around this lousy planet worth stealing," Kanjar said. "And super heroes like this one get in the way."

"That's Superman," said Kanjar's robotic first mate, El-Tak. "Superman gets his strength from the Earth's yellow sun. On Earth, he has incredible powers. Of course, outside the Earth's atmosphere —"

"Enough!" Kanjar said. "Don't be a fool. I know who Superman is. I tangled with him on Earth long before I acquired you."

"Well, there's no need to be rude about it," said El-Tak.

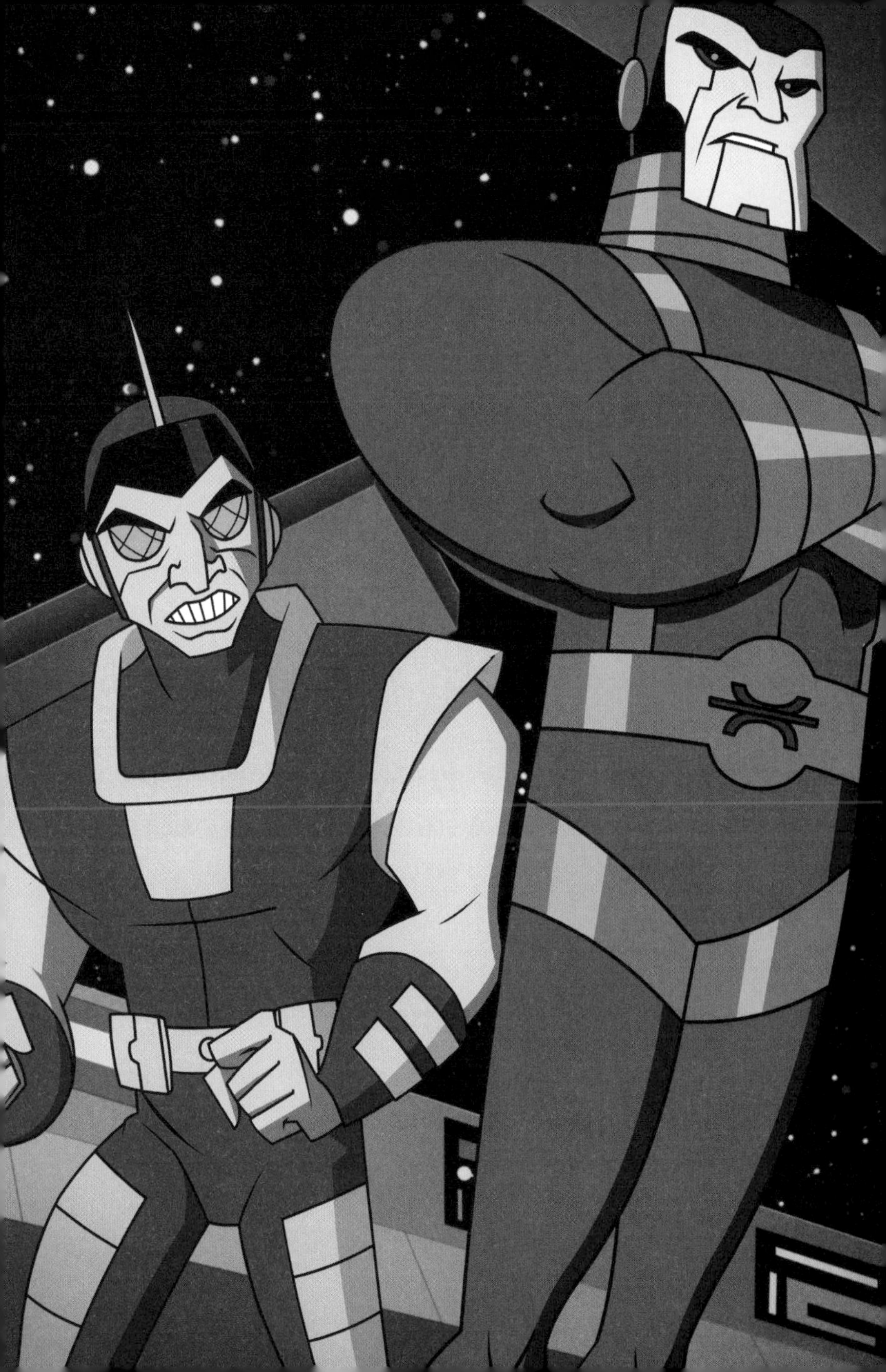

Kanjar ignored him. "See how our blasts just bounce off that ship Superman is carrying? Only one substance can deflect lasers like that — Leadellium. Very valuable stuff! I want it. El-Tak, send out the scavenger robots to take it!"

El-Tak didn't move. "Why aren't you sending out the scavengers?" screamed the space pirate.

"You didn't say 'Please,'" said the robot.

Kanjar Ro shook his head. He had won El-Tak from a space trader in a poker game. It was the worst bet Kanjar had ever won.

Unfortunately for Kanjar, his spacecraft was entirely robotic. There was no crew. El-Tak ran everything. Kanjar Ro gritted his teeth. It wasn't easy for the space pirate, but he managed to spit out "Please."

"See? That's not so hard, is it?" asked El-Tak. His tiny metal fingers danced across the ship's keyboard. **CLICK! CLICK!**

Across the outer hull of the pirate's warship, a dozen portals swirled open. Out of each opening flew a bug-like robot. The robots had sharp claws and metal teeth. They rocketed toward Superman and the rescue ship. **WHIR-WHIR-WHIR-WHIR!!**

"What were you saying about your greatest idea?" Superman asked Jimmy as the evil robots zoomed toward them.

"Um, I may have been wrong about that," said Jimmy. He looked out a portal and pointed. "What are those things?"

"Scavengers," said Superman grimly. "Which means that ship must be piloted by Kanjar Ro."

"There's a kangaroo flying that space ship?" questioned Jimmy.

"Kanjar Ro," Superman repeated. "The space pirate. I fought his scavengers when Kanjar tried to steal Metropolis's power plant. Those robots are tough."

The scavengers latched on to the rescue ship and started chomping on the hull.

"Hey, cut that out!" Jimmy cried from inside the ship. "Shoo! Shoo!"

Superman had his hands full carrying the ship. Even so, he was far from helpless.

The Man of Steel flipped up his visor and turned his heat vision on one of the scavengers. *BZZT!*

BOOM! It burst into a thousand flying fragments of metal. The rest of the bots stopped chomping on the rescue ship.

Superman smiled. Then suddenly, the robots turned their teeth on him!

The bug-like robots swarmed all over Superman. They were too close for him to blast with his heat vision. He needed his hands free.

"Hang on, Jimmy," shouted Superman. "I'll catch up with you in a minute."

"Huh?" yelled Jimmy. "What do you mean, 'catch up?'"

Before Jimmy could finish his sentence, Superman gripped the rescue ship tightly and then hurled it away! THWOOOOMMM!! The ship soared off at super-speed.

"Woooooaaaaaaaah!" cried Jimmy.

With the rescue ship continuing on toward Pluto, Superman turned his attention to the scavengers.

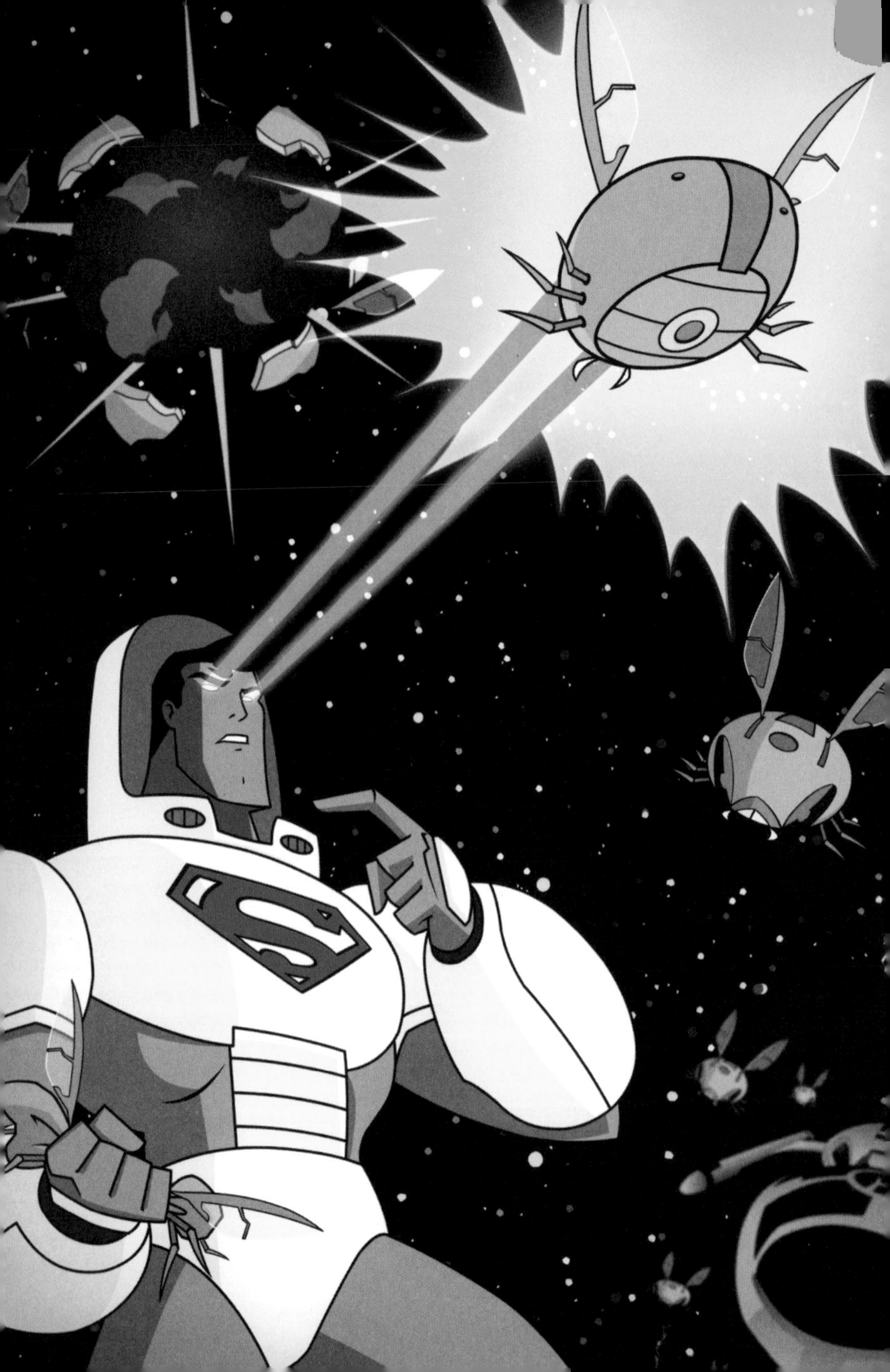

He grabbed the nearest one. **CRUNCH!** The robot crumbled in his grip. Then he turned and smashed another with a single punch. **WHAM!**

Superman was surprised. *When I fought Kanjar's scavengers in Metropolis,* he remembered, *they seemed a lot tougher.*

The last scavengers flew at Superman, gnashing their metal teeth. The Man of Steel blasted two with his heat vision, and then tore through the rest with his hands.

Inside his ship, Kanjar Ro couldn't believe what he was seeing.

"How can he be destroying my scavengers so easily?" Kanjar screamed.

"I tried to tell you before, but you just called me a fool," said El-Tak, frowning. "That hurt my feelings."

Kanjar grabbed the robot by its neck. "I'll hurt more than your feelings if you don't tell me what's happening out there!"

"Superman gets his strength from Earth's sun," burbled El-Tak. "On Earth, the atmosphere blocks much of the sun's rays. But outside the Earth's atmosphere —"

"I'm getting the full power of the sun," boomed Superman from just outside Kanjar's spacecraft. "Which makes me stronger than I am on Earth."

"Sorry for eavesdropping," Superman added. "I guess my super-hearing's more powerful too."

"Retreat!" yelped Kanjar Ro. "Get us out of here, El-Tak!"

"Let me help you with that," Superman said, smiling.

The Man of Steel grabbed Kanjar's ship.
Then he gave it a huge shove.

The pirate ship spun wildly off into
space.

"Aaaarggggh!!" screamed Kanjar
Ro inside the spinning ship. "El-Tak, do
something!"

"Not until you stop yelling," said El-Tak,
as he and Kanjar Ro spun off into the
darkness.

CHAPTER 3

THE DEPTHS OF SPACE

Superman caught up with Jimmy just as the rescue ship passed Jupiter. Jimmy felt the spacecraft accelerate when Superman started to push again. At this speed, they would reach Pluto in under an hour.

"Remind me to call you the next time I'm late for work," cracked Jimmy.

As they flew closer to Saturn, Superman pointed out Saturn's rings. Each ring was actually made up of millions of rocks and ice chunks that were spinning around the planet.

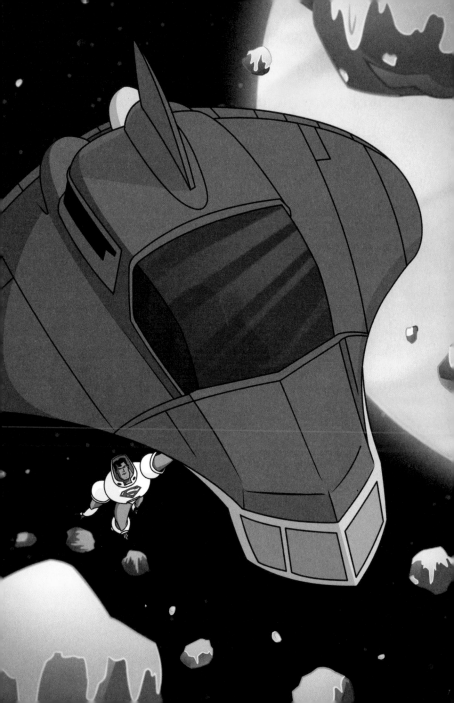

"It's too dangerous to get any closer," said Superman, adjusting the rescue ship's course. "Even I would have a hard time flying through all those rocks."

On the other side of the ship, Jimmy saw a beautiful streak of light burning across sky. It looked like an invisible brush was painting a blazing white arc against the solid black background of space.

"Look!" replied Jimmy. He pointed to the streak of light flying through the darkness. "It looks like that comet is flying right at us!"

Superman's eyes narrowed as he used his telescopic vision. "That's no comet," he said. "It's Kanjar Ro!"

Inside Kanjar's ship, the space pirate triple-checked El-Tak's calculations.

"This had better work, El-Tak," warned Kanjar Ro. "The scavengers should be able to defeat Superman this time . . . if your calculations aren't wrong."

"Not even a 'Thank You' for coming up with a plan to destroy Superman?" asked El-Tak. "Just because you're a space pirate doesn't mean you have to be rude."

"This Kanjar Ro guy just can't take a hint!" said Jimmy as the scavengers rocketed toward them. "Guess you're going to have to teach him another lesson!"

Superman nodded, and then turned his heat vision on the scavengers. The robots were only a hundred yards away, but for some reason, Superman's heat vision couldn't reach that far.

That's strange, thought Superman.

The scavengers swarmed toward him, grasping and clawing. Superman tried to crush one, but it was no use. He wasn't strong enough.

"Superman!" cried Jimmy. "What's wrong?"

Superman wasn't sure — and there was no time to figure it out. More and more scavengers poured out of Kanjar Ro's ship. They buzzed toward Superman, their hungry metal mouths ready for the attack.

There was only one thing Superman could do . . .

RUN!

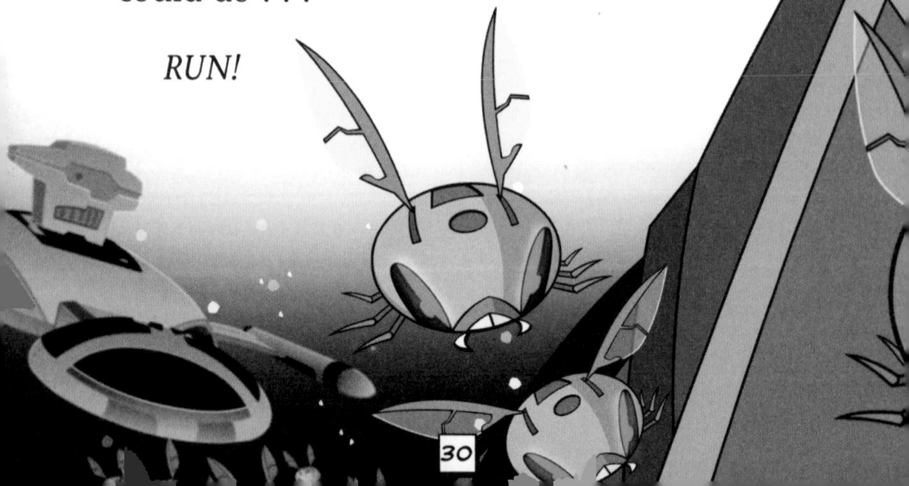

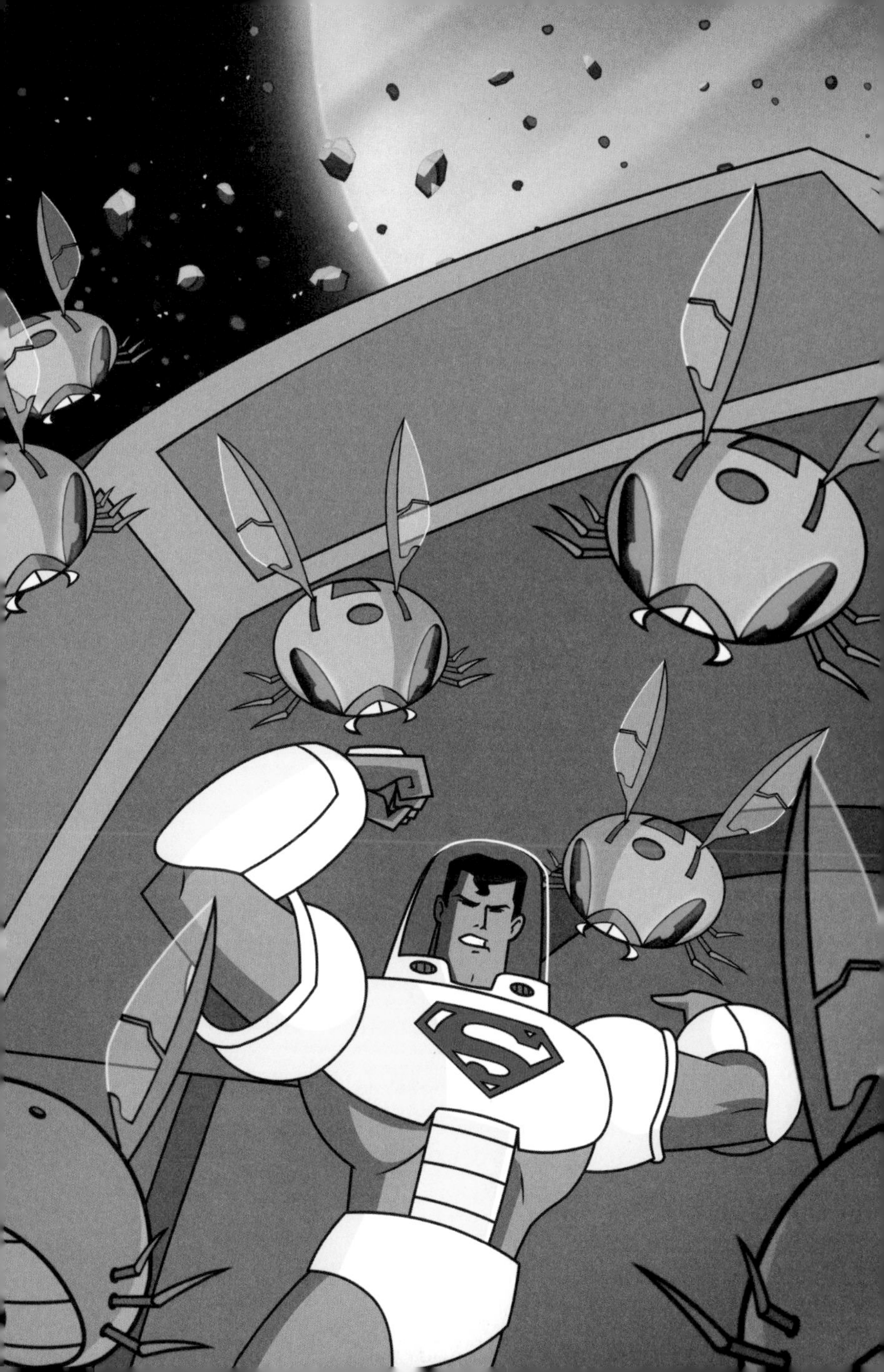

CHAPTER 4

SATURN'S RINGS

"Superman, stop!" cried Jimmy. "You're pushing us right into the rings of Saturn!"

Oomf! Jimmy fell to the floor as the rescue ship bounced off an ice-crusted rock swirling inside Saturn's rings.

"I thought you said it's dangerous with all these rocks in here," said Jimmy.

"It is," agreed Superman, "but it's more dangerous out there with those scavengers."

The rescue ship flew deeper into the rings.

Thousands of boulders the size of office buildings whipped around them. Superman quickly lost the scavengers in the swirling maze of rocks.

"Looks like we got away from them," said Jimmy. "I wonder how those creepy scavengers got so much stronger?"

"I don't think they did," replied Superman. "I think I got weaker."

"How?" replied Jimmy in disbelief.

"I get my powers from the sun," said Superman. "There's not much sunlight this deep in the solar system. That means I'm not able to draw as much energy from the sun as I normally do."

"Then we gotta go back to Earth!" said Jimmy. "If Kanjar Ro and his scavengers find us —" THWACK!

A huge chunk of rock smashed into the rescue ship's nose. **THUD! SLAM!** Two more rocks hit the hull.

"Jimmy! I can't see all the rocks ahead of us," Superman called out. "I need you to guide me."

"You want me to navigate?" sputtered Jimmy. "But I don't know anything about steering a space —"

Suddenly, Jimmy saw a rock flying right at him. "Left!" cried Jimmy. "Turn left!"

Superman banked the ship to the left, narrowly avoiding a collision.

"Looks like you're learning fast!" said Superman with a smile.

Just then, Jimmy saw Kanjar's warship flying toward them through Saturn's rings.

"What's he doing?" asked Jimmy. "No way he can pilot that giant ship through this maze. He'll smash into a rock for sure."

"I think he wants to!" said Superman.

Kanjar Ro's ship barreled toward an enormous rock. **KRAK!** It rammed the big boulder, sending it flying into two others. Those rocks then spun off and collided with several more. Soon, hundreds of icy rocks were flying wildly back and forth, bouncing off each other like balls on a pool table.

Before, it had been *almost* impossible to navigate between the rocks. But now it *was* impossible!

"Get us out of here!" yelled Jimmy.

Superman sped up. He pushed the ship straight through the thick swirl of rocks.

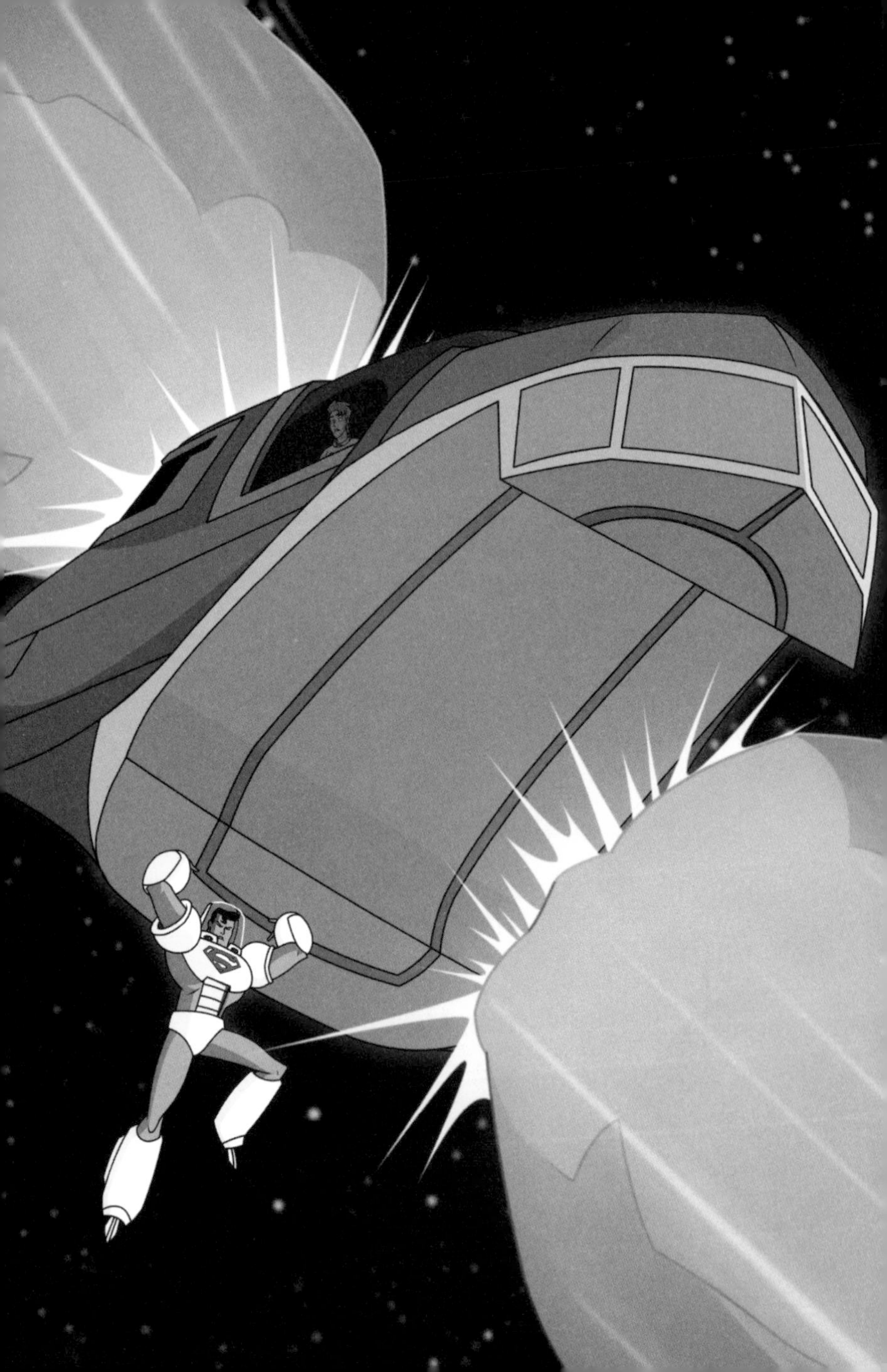

POW! Stones the size of garbage trucks slammed into the rescue ship. They couldn't hurt the ship, but Superman didn't want to find out what would happen if one struck him instead.

"Look out, Superman!" cried Jimmy.

Superman dodged the massive rock heading right toward him. Then, suddenly they were out of Saturn's rings. They'd made it, but there was no time to celebrate.

"That detour through the rings cost us minutes we don't have," said Superman. "We're going to have to take a shortcut . . . through Neptune."

"Wait a minute," replied Jimmy. "*Through* a planet?"

"Neptune's a gas giant," explained Superman.

"It's not solid like Earth," he continued. "I can fly straight through it."

"Hang on," exclaimed Jimmy. "Do you really think that's possible?"

"Don't worry," said Superman. "Not even Neptune's core can melt through the rescue ship's Leadellium hull."

"What about you?" asked Jimmy. "Even if you're not as strong as you usually are, you'll still be fine . . . right?"

"We're about to find out," said Superman. He guided the ship toward Neptune. The deep blue planet was dotted with giant storms across its surface.

Superman and the ship smashed through Neptune's outer atmosphere. For the first time since leaving Earth, Superman and Jimmy had left the void of space.

Now they were someplace a lot deadlier!

Superman and Jimmy found themselves in the middle of a storm the size of North America. Thousand-mile-an-hour winds threw them back and forth. BOOM! KRAK! Giant spears of lightning crashed over them. SPLASH! Acid rain lashed across the ship and poured down over Superman.

Down, down, he pushed the ship — straight toward the center of the gas giant. The core was liquid. It was as thick as glue. It was also hot enough to melt iron in an instant. Superman scanned the rescue ship's Leadellium hull. The heat had no effect on the super-strong metal.

Superman hoped he would hold up as well. The heat of Neptune's core danced across his arms and legs. Suddenly, Superman felt something unfamiliar.

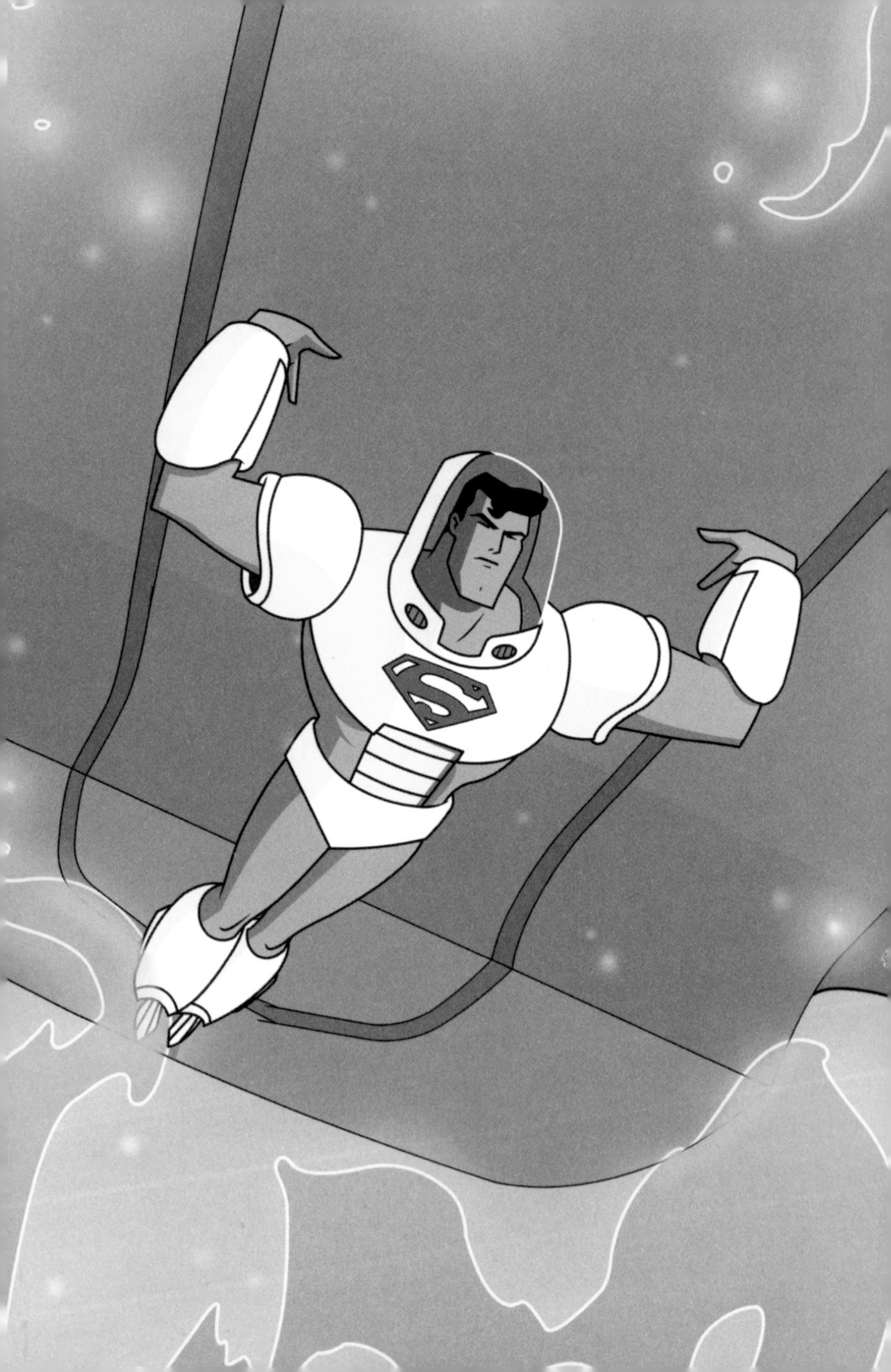

It took him a moment to recognize it.

It was pain!

Just when he thought he couldn't take any more . . . **WHOOOOSH!** Superman and the ship burst out the other side of the liquid core. They zoomed straight through Neptune's atmosphere and back out into space.

"Woo-hoo!" shouted Jimmy excitedly. "We made it! I knew you could do it!"

Exhausted, Superman nodded. He scanned the skies ahead of them.

Pluto, and the stranded astronauts, were almost within reach!

The only thing between them and their destination was . . . Kanjar Ro!

CHAPTER 5

PLUTO

Kanjar Ro's warship barreled toward Superman and Jimmy. "At first, I just wanted the Leadellium in that ship's hull," shrieked Kanjar inside his cockpit. "But now I'm going to take a greater prize — Superman himself!"

After the journey through the rocky rings of Saturn, and the boiling liquid core of Neptune, Superman was exhausted. Pluto was right there in front of him. Superman still had time to rescue the astronauts, but he was weaker than ever.

Hardly any light reached this far from the sun.

I flew all the way across the solar system, thought Superman. *I can't fail now!*

As the last of Kanjar Ro's scavengers rushed toward him, Superman tried to blast them with his heat vision. *FZZZT!*

Nothing happened. Superman punched the closest scavenger, but it kept coming. The bug-like bots swarmed over him. Superman couldn't hold onto the rescue ship. He could only watch as it drifted away from Pluto — with Jimmy inside it!

It was the last thing he saw before the scavengers knocked the super hero out.

In the rescue ship's cockpit, Jimmy saw the scavengers drag Superman toward Kanjar Ro's spacecraft.

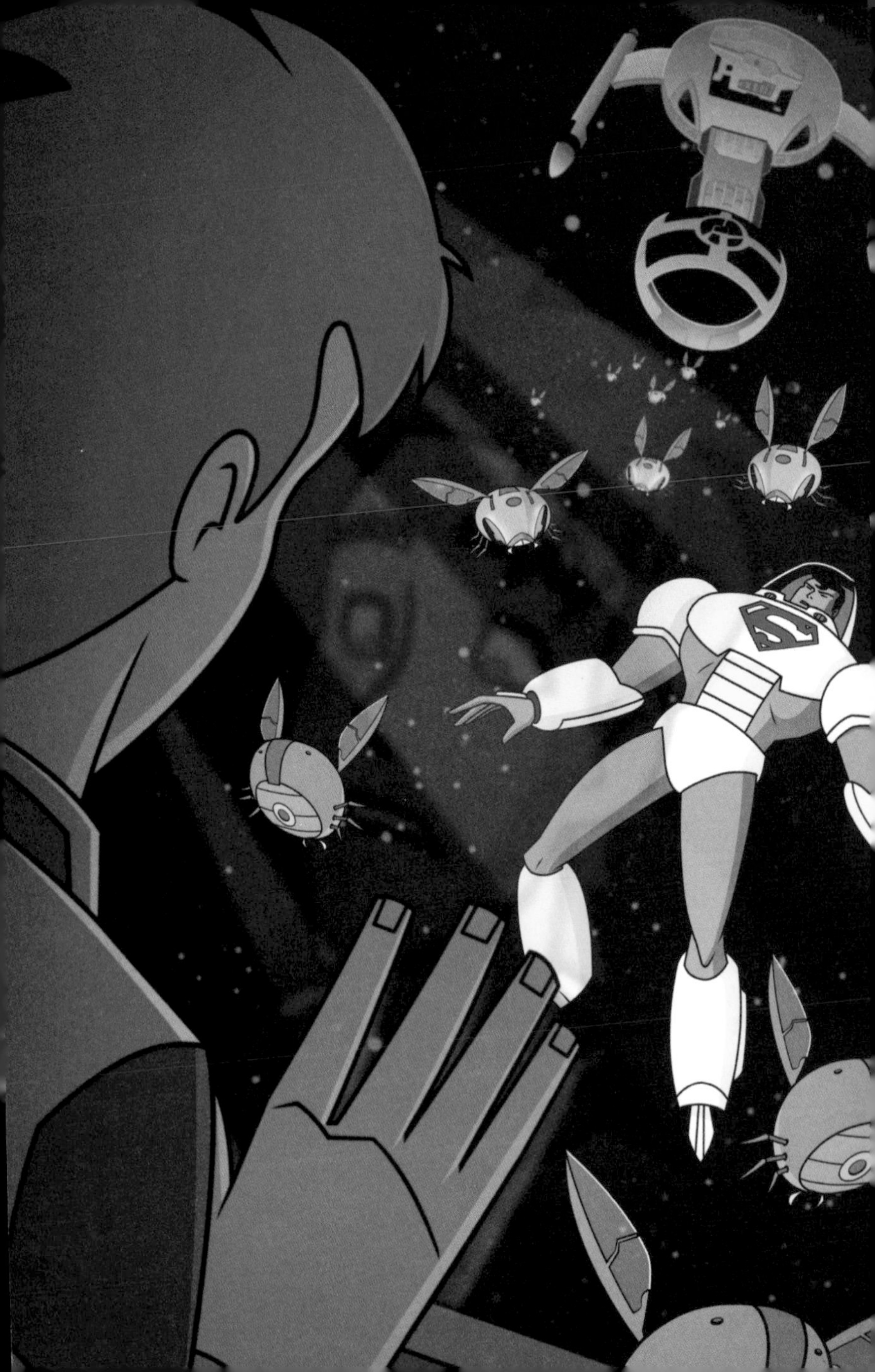

"No!" Jimmy cried, slamming his fist down in anger. **CLICK!** His hand landed on the rescue ship's control panel. It whirred to life.

"Uh-oh," croaked Jimmy.

Suddenly, the rescue ship shot forward.

"Wooaaaaaaah!" cried Jimmy as he smashed into the scavengers at full speed. The ship's Leadellium hull did the rest — crunching and breaking the robots into hundreds of metal shards. Superman floated free of the scavengers as Jimmy roared through them.

Jimmy was still traveling incredibly fast, and Kanjar Ro's warship was right in front of him. The two ships were going to crash! "Which button turns this thing off?" Jimmy moaned.

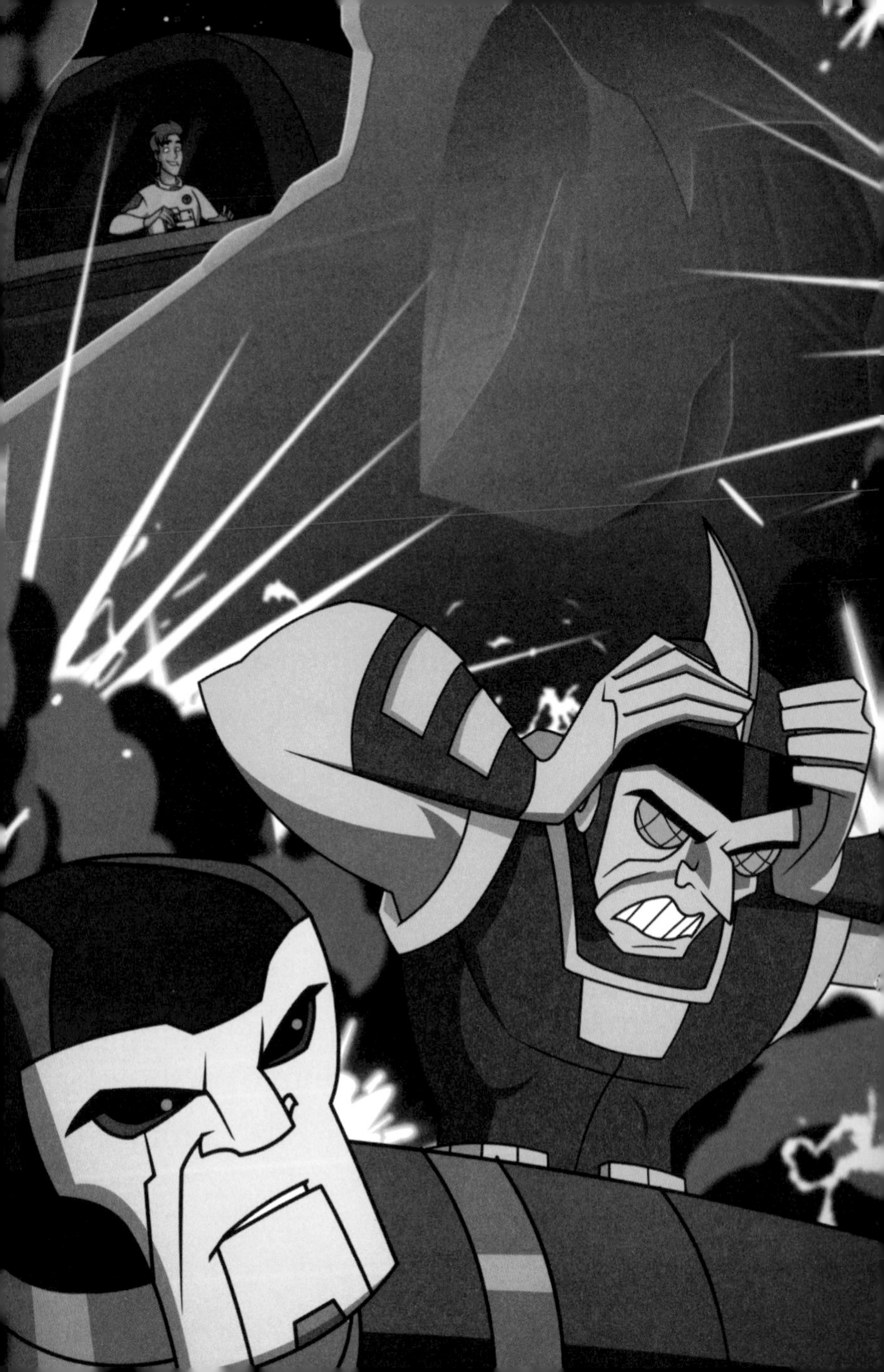

Jimmy covered his eyes as the two massive spaceships collided. He was sure that this was the end. **CRASH!!**

And it was . . . for Kanjar Ro's ship.

The indestructible rescue ship crunched the space pirate's vessel into a pile of metal. Its engines destroyed, it floated away with Kanjar Ro and El-Tak trapped inside.

"Yeargggghhh!!!" yelled Kanjar Ro.

"Again with the yelling," said El-Tak. "I really don't know why I put up with it."

As the two of them drifted off helplessly, one thought consumed the space pirate. Some day, somehow, Kanjar Ro would escape. And when he did, there was one thing he would do, no matter what it took.

He was going to get a new robot assistant.

*   *   *

Later, at the S.T.A.R. Labs Space Center, the astronauts exited the rescue ship to thunderous applause. Jimmy followed them. He was glad to be back on Earth — until the general grabbed him by the collar.

"I want a word with you," said the general.

"We all do," agreed Superman, as he followed Jimmy out of the ship.

Jimmy winced. *Here it comes,* he thought.

"And that word," Superman continued, "is 'Thanks!'"

"None of us would be here if Jimmy Olsen hadn't stowed away on the ship," Superman added.

Everyone cheered.

Superman put a hand on Jimmy's shoulder. "Not bad for your first trip to space," he said, grinning.

"Maybe so," said Jimmy, "but if I have anything to say about it, it's also going to be my last!"

DAILY PLANET

FROM THE DESK OF CLARK KENT

WHO IS KANJAR RO?

Although Kanjar Ro has no superpowers of his own, he is more than capable of spreading destruction and suffering wherever he goes. He travels the universe as a space pirate, acquiring technology and resources by stealing from other space travelers. His stockpile of stolen alien weapons allows him to overpower lesser-equipped foes. Kanjar Ro is also a brilliant strategist. On several occasions, he has been able to defeat his enemies, and take over entire planets, through careful planning and clever tricks.

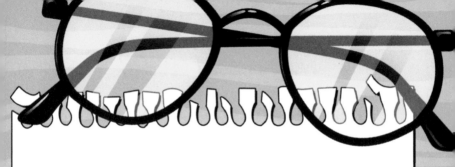

- Kanjar Ro possesses an advanced piece of alien weaponry called the Gamma Gong. It is capable of paralyzing anyone, including the Man of Steel. It is also capable of brainwashing an individual into doing Kanjar Ro's bidding.

- Having seen many different kinds of alien technology during his interstellar travels, Kanjar Ro is capable of quickly learning how to use any type of weapon or spaceship he comes across.

- Kanjar Ro once brainwashed the entire Justice League with his Gamma Gong. He used the super heroes in an attempt to take over several planets, but they eventually broke free. Always scheming, Kanjar Ro was still able to evade capture.

- Kanjar Ro was able to get his hands on a piece of technology called the Energi-Rod. The device allows him to teleport and fly, and also grants him the ability to communicate across great distances.

BIOGRAPHIES

Scott Sonneborn has written 20 books, one circus (for Ringling Bros. Barnum & Bailey), and a bunch of TV shows. He's been nominated for an Emmy and spent three very cool years working at DC Comics. He lives in Los Angeles with his wife and their two sons.

Dan Schoening was born in Victoria, B.C. Canada. From an early age, Dan has had a passion for animation and comic books. Currently, Dan does freelance work in the animation and game industry and spends a lot of time with his lovely little daughter, Paige.

GLOSSARY

accelerate (ak-SEL-uh-rate)—to increase speed

acquired (uh-KWIRED)—obtain or get something

deflect (di-FLEKT)—to make something go in a
different direction

enormous (i-NOR-muhss)—extremely large

fragment (FRAG-muhnt)—a small piece or part
that has broken away from the whole

grimly (GRIM-lee)—in a gloomy, stern, or
unpleasant way

massive (MASS-iv)—large, heavy, and solid

propelling (pruh-PEL-ing)—driving or pushing
something forward

shard (SHARD)—a jagged piece of something

stranded (STRAND-id)—left behind

void (VOID)—an empty or barren space

DISCUSSION QUESTIONS

1. If you could have any of Superman's superpowers, which one would you choose?

2. Is Jimmy a hero for helping to save those astronauts, or should he have been punished for sneaking onto the ship? Why?

3. Kanjar Ro makes his living by stealing things from others. Is it ever okay to steal? Explain.

WRITING PROMPTS

1. At first, Superman was upset that Jimmy stowed away on the ship. But later, Jimmy proved to be very helpful. Write about a time when something you thought would be bad turned out to be good.

2. Kanjar Ro's scavengers are robotic insects, and El-Tak is his android first mate. Think up your own mechanical servant. What does it look like? What can it do? Draw a picture of your robot.

3. Kanjar Ro and El-Tak don't get along very well. Have you ever had to work with someone you didn't like? Write about it.

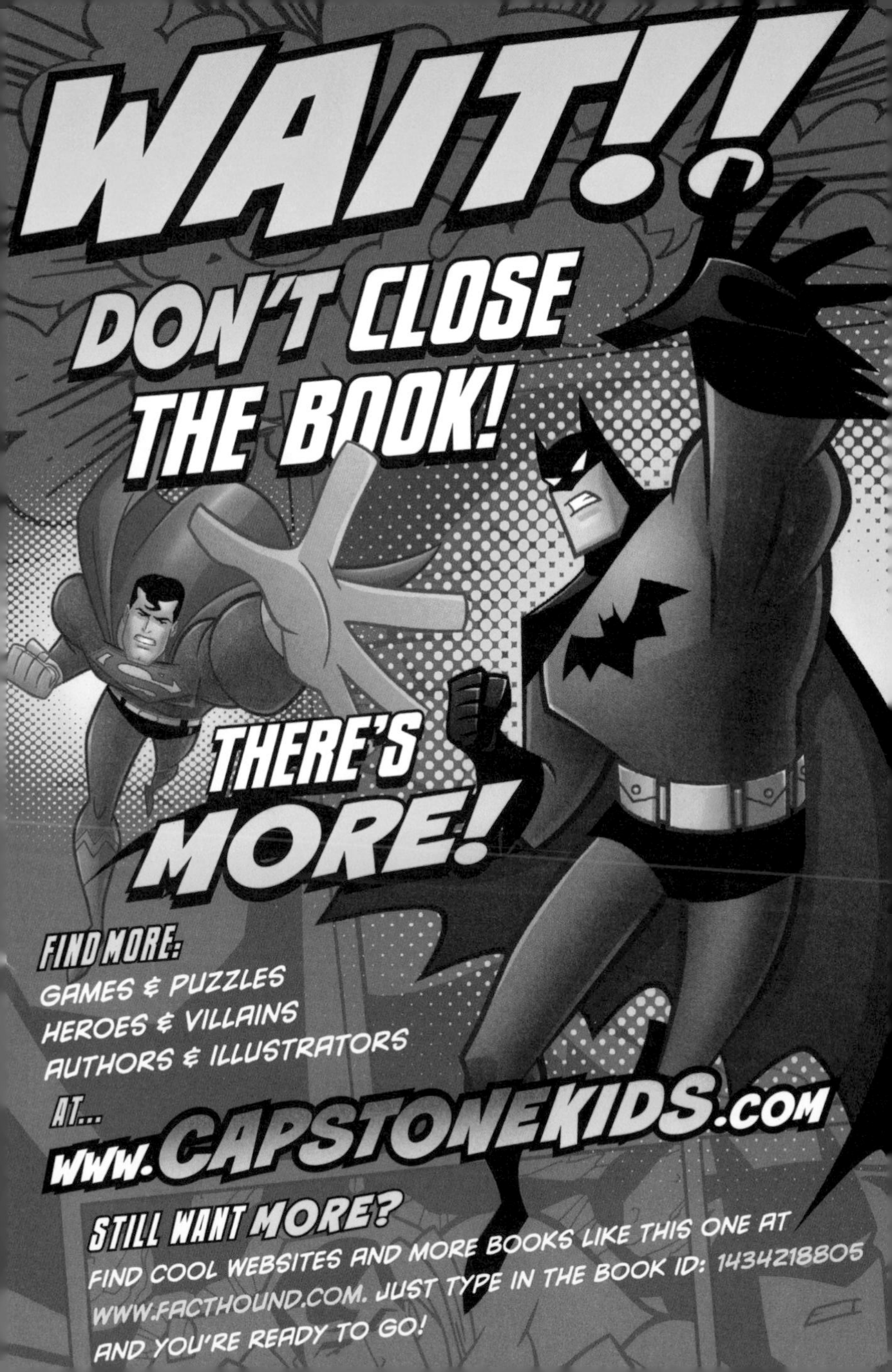
WAIT!!
DON'T CLOSE THE BOOK!
THERE'S MORE!
FIND MORE:
GAMES & PUZZLES
HEROES & VILLAINS
AUTHORS & ILLUSTRATORS
AT...
WWW.CAPSTONEKIDS.COM
STILL WANT MORE?
FIND COOL WEBSITES AND MORE BOOKS LIKE THIS ONE AT
WWW.FACTHOUND.COM. JUST TYPE IN THE BOOK ID: 1434218805
AND YOU'RE READY TO GO!

MORE NEW SUPERMAN ADVENTURES!

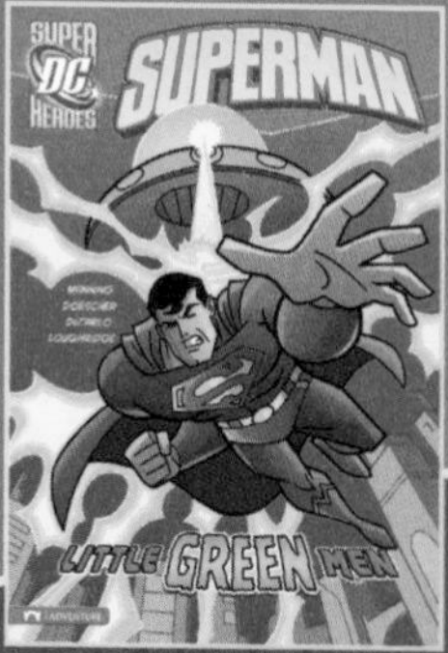
SUPER DC HEROES
SUPERMAN
LITTLE GREEN MEN

LITTLE GREEN MEN

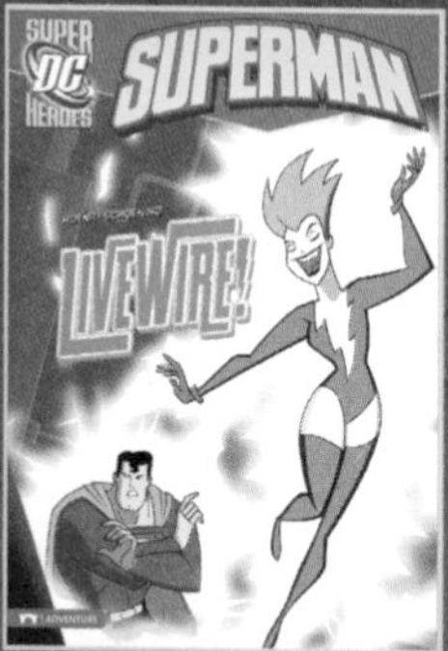
SUPER DC HEROES
SUPERMAN
LIVEWIRE!

LIVEWIRE!

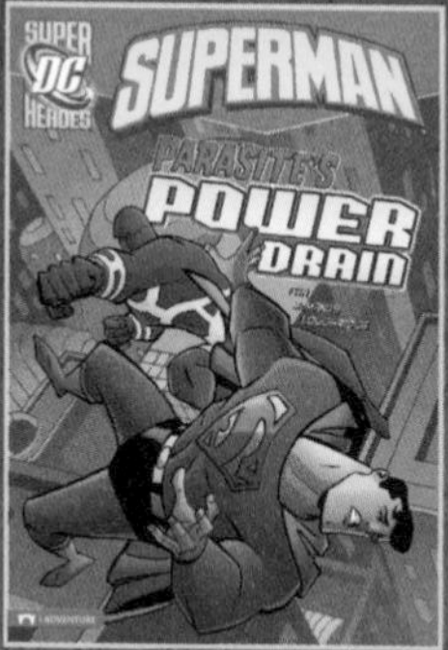
SUPER DC HEROES
SUPERMAN
PARASITE'S POWER DRAIN

PARASITE'S POWER DRAIN

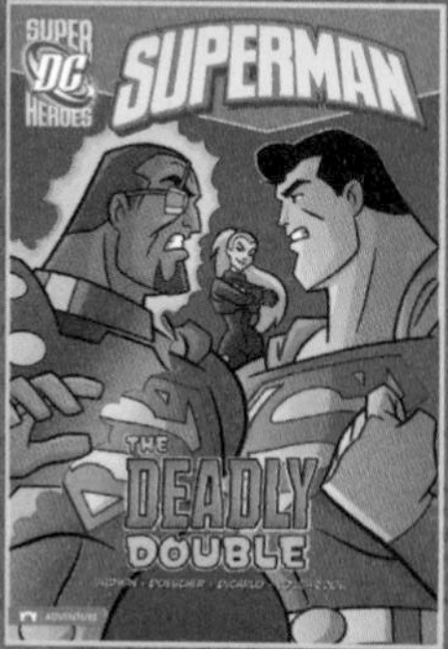
SUPER DC HEROES
SUPERMAN
THE DEADLY DOUBLE

THE DEADLY DOUBLE

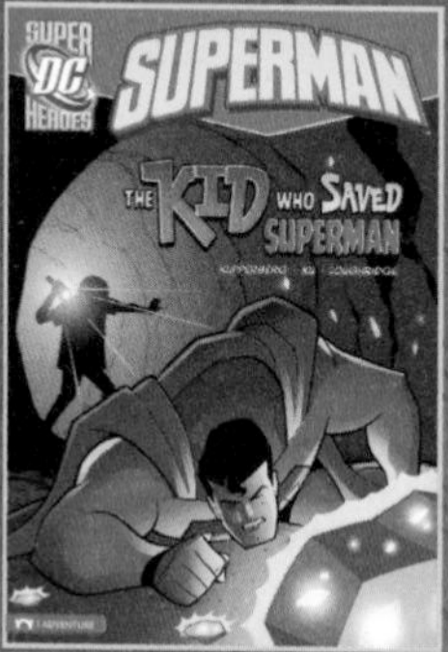
SUPER DC HEROES
SUPERMAN
THE KID WHO SAVED SUPERMAN

THE KID WHO SAVED SUPERMAN

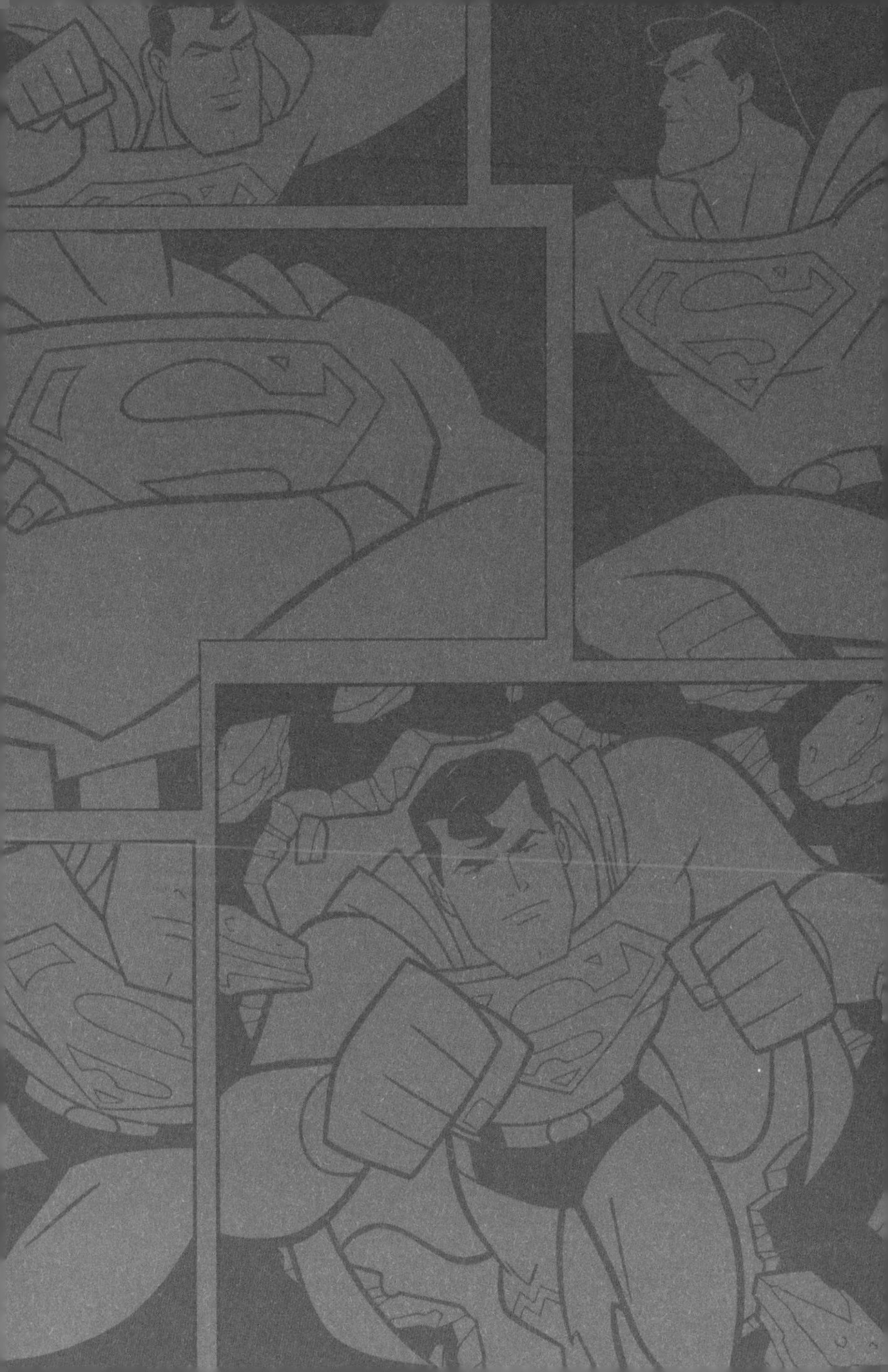

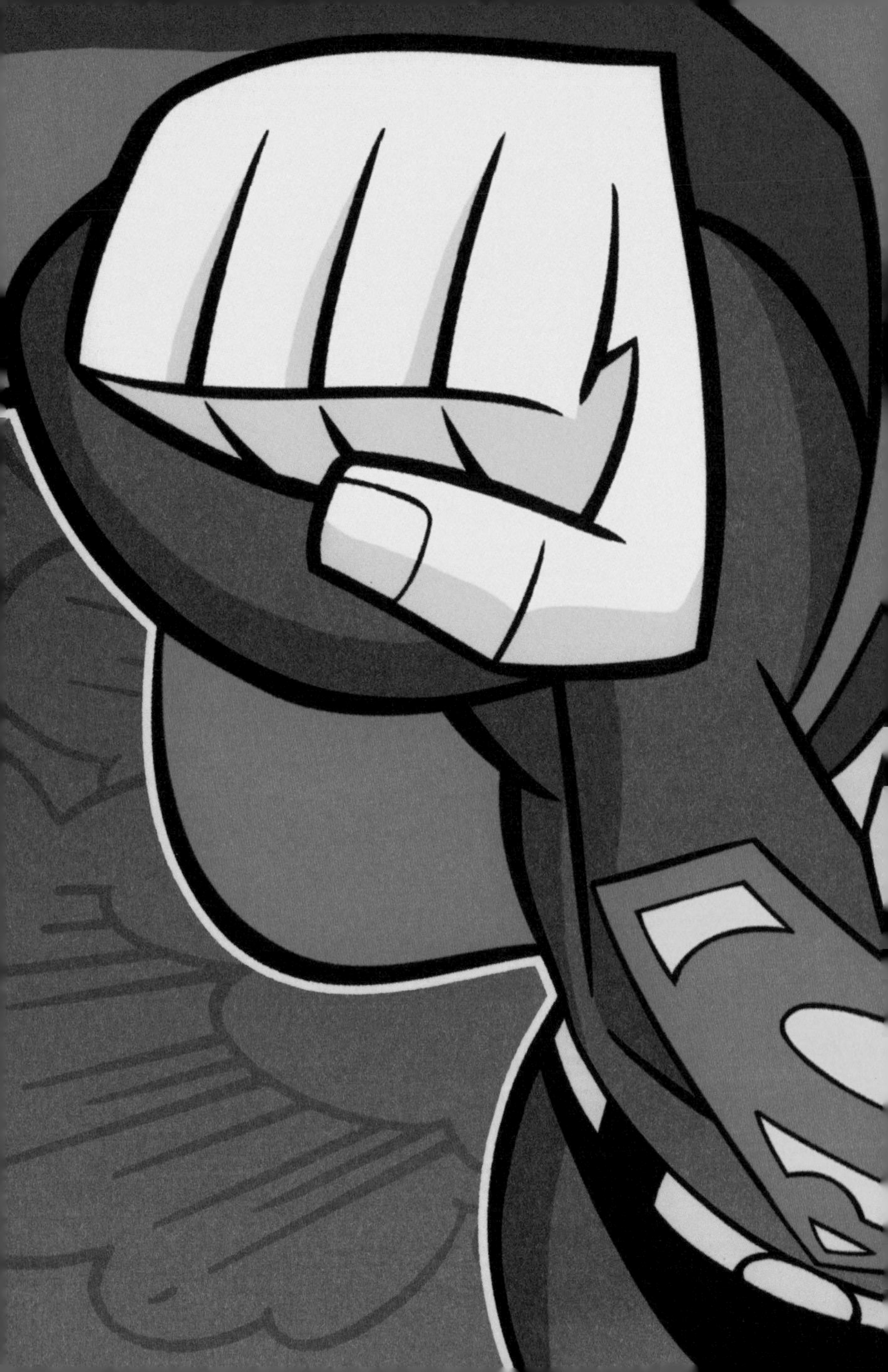

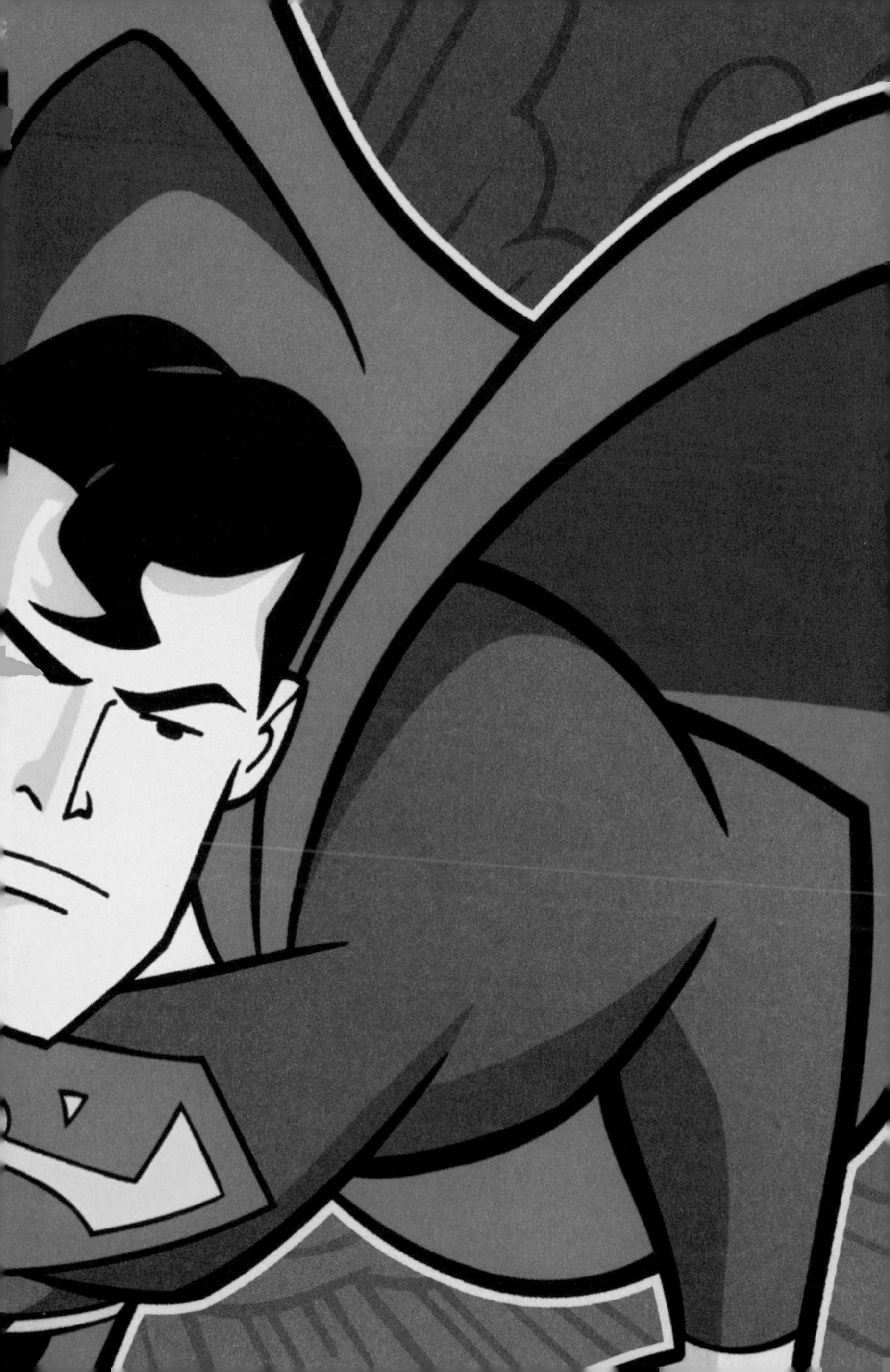